A VERY BRAVE Witch

Alison McGHEE

Harry BLISS

A PAULA WISEMAN BOOK
Simon & Schuster Books for Young Readers
New York London Toronto Sydney

SIMON & SCHUSTER BOOKS FOR YOUNG READERS

An imprint of Simon & Schuster Children's Publishing Division

1230 Avenue of the Americas, New York, New York 10020

Text copyright © 2006 by Alison McGhee

Illustrations copyright © 2006 by Harry Bliss

SIMON & SCHUSTER BOOKS FOR YOUNG READERS is a trademark of Simon & Schuster.

Book design by Einav Aviram

Hand lettering by Paul Colin

The illustrations for this book are rendered in black ink and

watercolor on Arches 90 lb. watercolor paper.

Manufactured in China

2 4 6 8 10 9 7 5 3 1

Library of Congress Cataloging-in-Publication Data

McGhee, Alison, 1960-

A very brave witch / Alison McGhee ; illustrated by Harry Bliss.-- 1st ed.

p. cm.

"A Paula Wiseman book."

Summary: A young witch describes what she does on Halloween, her favorite holiday.

ISBN-13: 978-0-689-86730-9 (isbn-13)

ISBN-10: 0-689-86730-1 (isbn-10)

[1. Halloween—Fiction. 2. Witches—Fiction.] I. Bliss, Harry, 1964-, ill. II. Title.

PZ7.M4784675Som 2006

[E]—dc22

2005016108

To Holly McGhee—A. M.
For Charley and Ben Bliss—H. B.

Most humans do not wear pointy hats.

Humans are rarely known to cackle.

HA, HA, HA, HA

Nothing too bad, except, you know... the green thing.